For Fallon, my perfect piglet,
Jean, my persevering publisher,
and Brenda, my partner in rhyme.
—C. T.

To Oliver Stanley and Oliver Riley Deas.
And to Jean, for all her inspiration and support.
—R. D.

A FEIWEL AND FRIENDS BOOK
An Imprint of Macmillan

COCK-A-DOODLE DANCE! Text copyright © 2012 by Christine Tricarico.
Illustrations copyright © 2012 by Rich Deas.
All rights reserved.
Printed in China by Macmillan Production (Asia) Ltd.,
Kwun Tong, Kowloon, Hong Kong. Supplier Code: 10
For information, address Feiwel and Friends,
175 Fifth Avenue, New York, N.Y. 10010.

Library of Congress Cataloging-in-Publication Data Available

ISBN: 978-0-312-38251-3

Book design by Rich Deas and April Ward

Feiwel and Friends logo designed by Filomena Tuosto

First Edition: 2012

1   3   5   7   9   10   8   6   4   2

mackids.com

COCK-A-
DOODLE
DANCE!

by Christine Tricarico

illustrated by Rich Deas

FEIWEL AND FRIENDS · NEW YORK

In rootin', tootin' Texas
is a gloomy, grouchy farm
where animals work overtime
and life has lost its charm.

"Cock-a-Doodle DULL!"

The Rooster wakes his farm at five
to start their working day,
but **layin' eggs** and **makin' milk**
leaves little time for play. . . .

Rooster catches a **jitterbug**
that **shakes** the barnyard beams.
He slicks his ruffled feathers back,
he **shimmies** on the crows.

This jitterbug's contagious;
boogie fever's catchin' on.
The others follow Rooster's lead
to doodle-dance at dawn.

You won't see cows a-milkin'
or the chickens layin' eggs.
Instead, you'll witness **bovines bow**
and poultries' **prancin' legs.**

The animals love groovin'
as they pivot, pounce, and prance,
but no one cares that work's not done,
since all they do is **dance**!

By evening,
ducks are dancin'
under starry,
shadowed nights.

And turkeys
tango wango,
reaching
stratospheric
heights.

The chickens do
the **cha-cha**,
as the dogs begin
ballet,

and **shimmy** sheep
don't stop their
swing until
the light of day.

"COCK-A-DOODLE GET DOWN!"

As sunlight fills the morning sky,
the cats still need to doze.
Yet, Rooster starts a **RUMBA**
in his finest conga clothes.

So, grazing goats or shearin' sheep
are not what you will find.
Instead, the cows start **Clogging**
like they've lost their moo-moo minds!

"Cock-a-Mooodle
YEEE-HAA!"

By noon, the piglets' polka pies
are hitting heifer heads.
The cows can't nap with crusty calves
and filthy, dirty beds.

Soon, piggies plop and cows collapse!
The groggy goats can't graze
because there's been a nonstop bop
for almost two whole days!

So, Rooster rests the whole next day.
No "cock-a-doodle do!"
He doesn't move a muscle
'til a quarter after two.

"Cock-a-Doodle SNOOOZZE!"

He's finally roused by fed-up crowds
led by a **cranky cow**.
"We have to tell you something
and we have to say it **now**....

Our chickens' eggs are scrambled.
Drowsy dogs have lost their sheep
and buttermilk is curdled from the
cattle's lack of sleep."

"This barnyard's bushed," the pigs profess,
"from dancin' round the clock.
With broken eggs and sour milk,
we're now a laughingstock!"

Rooster takes a look around
at the cock-a-doodled mess.
"Our barnyard is a
hodgepodge heap,
I really must confess."

"We'll fix our farm,"
he proudly crows!
"And clean our sticky sties.
Then only doodle-dance at dusk
beneath the starlit skies."

"Cock-a-
Doodle
CLEAN UP!"

When morning
comes, the Rooster
wakes with

"Cock-a-Doodle   DO!"

The piglets scrub their muddy mess
and clean the calves up, too.

The cows make milk and hens lay eggs.
(They finally got some sleep.)
The turkeys get their **gobble** back
and dogs have found their sheep.

"Gobble Gobble Gobble Gobble!"

When chicken chores and turkey tasks
and barnyard jobs are through,
the animals can **belly dance**
and even **dipsy-doo**.

"**COCK-a-Doodle DANCE PARTY!**"

All play, no work, is just as bad as working **night** and **day**. Now critters lead a balanced life, but much to their **dismay** . . .

the farmer and his wife
have caught the jumpin' jitterbug,
they two-step, boogie woogie,
and they really cut a rug.

They stop their plows for polka,
leaving housework incomplete
because they've flown their kitchen coop
to waltz in fields of wheat!

"Cock-a-Doodle
YAA-HOO!"

Learn a bit about the DANCES.

Belly dancing—a Middle Eastern dance where dancers, usually females, make movements with their hips and stomach area.

Cha-Cha—an exciting Latin dance with repeated rhythm and foot movements which started in the 1950s.

Clogging—a dance requiring special shoes with metal taps on them that uses stomps, taps, and other rhythmic steps. Clogging started in the Blue Ridge Mountain area.

Hula—a Hawaiian dance that tells stories through the movements of arms and legs. The basic step in the hula dance is called the chassé where the hips sway and swing.

Conga—a Latin American dance of three steps and a kick by people in single file.

Jitterbug—became popular in the 1920s and was also known as the "Hop" and "Swing." This dance was usually performed to jazz music.

Promenade—a V-shaped dance position where partners move forward in the same direction toward the opening end of the "V."

Polka—a fun dance that started in Bohemia. Couples hop, skip, and step to lively music.